CLAIRAUDIENCE

J. C. F. Grumbine

Pharos Books

ISBN: 978-93-58049-10-7
eISBN: 978-93-58049-21-3

©Publisher

Publisher: Pharos Books (P) Ltd.
Plot No.-63, Main Mother Dairy Road
Pandav Nagar, East Delhi-110092
Phone: 011-40395855, +4049916623
WhatsApp: +91 8368220032
E-mail: sales@pharosbooks.in
Website: www.pharosbooks.in
First Edition: 2024

Printed By: Sushma Book Binding House, Okhla
Industrial Area, Phase II, New Delhi-110020

CLAIRAUDIENCE
By J. C. F. GRUMBINE

CONTENTS

FOREWORD

To those who know nothing of, or who doubt everything, about the spirit world, this series of teachings will have no meaning; but to the students of psychical phenomena and supernormal development this practical treatise will be timely and providential. No work of inspiration is sent to earth without a purpose. The needs, the aspirations, the sufferings of humanity evoke the ministrations of spirits and depth and height meet, as it were, by a law of cause and effect, science has not as yet explained.

The new or supernormal psychology is rapidly winning favor, and is supplanting the old and abnormal. External means of communication between men are pointing to interior means of communication between spirits and mankind, and what telepathy previses as possible between men on the material plane, clairsentience, clairvoyance and clairaudience prove is practical between incarnate and excarnate spirits.

Spirit is at the base of all communication and communion, whether outward or material, or mental or spiritual.

Acts of the supernormal powers of the incarnate spirits are no more wonderful or remarkable than the clairvoyant visions and clairaudient messages afforded us by excarnate spirits, whom the world calls "dead". Wireless wires reach from our sight and hearing to unseen, silent operators on the excarnate (spirit) side of life. The joy of discovering this is only exceeded by the knowledge of the actual daily communion and communication with the unseen immortals! Think of it! Where are they? Do they suffer, or are they happy? Do they live and love us still? Go into the silence! Tick off a message to the spirit operators by telepathy; or vision the clairvoyant sight on to the supernormal plane where your deceased loved ones live; or take up the spirit telephone, called clairaudience, and listen. Listen deeply, reverently. A message thrills by sympathy or love over the unseen wires, called psychic filaments; a vision of your dear ones dawns on your mind as out of the mystery of the inner mental darkness; or the angel voice of a dear companion, gone as you thought forever, whispers close to your mind, and seems to be heard, often accompanied with a cold breath pressing against your face, or wells up in the midst of your vocal organs and the throat. And this is the greatest discovery and mystery of life, far more valuable because of the superlatively beneficent service in the human and divine sense, to every human being.

All can and therefore should feel, see, and hear super-normally, all can and therefore should receive and send messages from the earth to the spirit world.

As the book on Clairvoyance, by J. C. F. Grumbine, revealed the law and science of supernormal seeing, seeing spiritually into this as well as the spirit world, so this book reveals the law and science of supernormal hearing, hearing spiritually messages from this and the spirit world.

Study and apply the teachings, the results follow.

● ● ●

1

What Clairaudience Is

Technically speaking, clairaudience is, in the terminology of the new psychology, the supernormal as well as superphysical power of clear or spiritual hearing. Normal audience or hearing is hearing *sounds,* and by them interpreting *thoughts** Supernormal hearing, or clairaudience, is hearing thoughts unmanifest or unexpressed in sounds. Normal hearing deals with thought forms or pictures created by sound waves or vibrations; while clairaudience deals with vibrations which transcend the normal scale or spectrum. It is specifically the language of the spirit, or one of the spiritual modes of communication and communion between excarnate and incarnate spirits. For since we are spirits, whether in or out of the physical body, we have access to spiritual as well as material means of communication.

Now it would be remarkable if sometime in our life we did not hear a voice, which spoke to our inmost nature, when no one was near,—a voice which seemed a warning and to pressage disaster, and was actually followed by bad news! How many have not asked "who's there!" when suddenly halted in their course by a voice which seemed to issue out of the invisible air? In most instances, this voice is that of a spirit who speaks to the clairaudient and so startles the sleep walker, called man, as he dreams his mortal dreams of existence. Paul heard this voice when on the road to Damascus. Jesus cried out, "Saul, Saul why persecutest thou me?". And throughout the history of Israel as recorded in the Bible the "thus saith the Lord", is proof of the frequency of the clairaudient voice.

That a spirit can so address a mortal is not strange from a Biblical, if not from the view point of the new psychology and Spiritualism. In fact, one need not seek for evidences of the clairaudient power and voice outside of our own generation and the annals of the times, for it is far more common among mankind today than the most enthusiastic advocates believe. Of course, those who enjoy clairaudient voices are not always publishing the fact in the newspapers, nor are they confiding their extraordinary and sacred experiences to the scoffer or the superstitious, nor to their most intimate friends, because they do not wish to be judged insane by the ignorant or worldly wise. Still in our very large and extended acquaintance with all sorts of people, we have met hundreds who when they were pressed to speak openly and without reserve, or when all fear of ridicule was removed, confessed as did the great Greek philosopher, Socrates, that they had always been guided and inspired by a clairaudient power, or voice, (demon, as Socrates called it, from the Greek dunamis which means a force or power). And this same Socrates bears the historical reputation of being the wisest of men.

Lest some agnostic may think that such a voice is purely fictitious or imaginary, concrete facts in the life of the intelligence who speaks are often cited to show that the voice is excarnate or supernatural, belonging to a separate entity, who speaks, as it were, from another world. Much proof is accessible to convince the doubter that such bodiless voices have been traced to spirit people,— men, women and children who once lived on earth, but who now enjoy in the spirit world a free life and a more enlarged power of individual and psychic freedom and initiative. Not only is this so, but these spirit people have given facts in their lives which have been verified in every particular, so that whatever the skeptic thought the voice might be, the evidence of the intelligence back of the voices could not be denied. And these facts are all the more credible because experienced by thousands.

The independent voices differ from the clairaudient. The clairaudient voices are always from within the soul, (spirit communing with spirit) and are bodiless or soundless, so that only the clairaudient can hear them. While the independent voices are vocalized and externalized into the air, so that the sense of hearing can apprehend them.

A mortal can address an immortal and an immortal can address a mortal clairaudiently. The law permits clairaudient intercommunications from the material to the ethereal planes and vice versa. Clairaudience is the direct, and vocal utterence and audience to vocal utterance, the indirect means of spirit communication. And yet clairaudience is such spirit and spiritual communion as thought and language can express and manifest, and yet they cannot explain.

Often one's attention will be suddenly and startlingly arrested by a clairaudient spirit voice, spoken and heard so loudly that one may be surprised not to see a mortal standing near; or a voice may be heard so loudly in one's sleep as to awaken one, and yet no one physically visible called. These clairaudient voices are so subjectified as to make them seem objective or material, the impression of sound being registered on the objective mind as such sufficiently through the subjective, spiritual process as to make it seem physically audible.

So much for the facts of clairaudience. Let the student now apply the following experiment.

EXPERIMENT 1

Sit in a subdued light, and at a time when there is the least noise or possible interruption. Sympathetically dwell upon some spirit who is very near and dear. Have a paper pad and pencil handy. Listen for impressions, note them down on paper. Follow this habit daily and observe how touches as of a feather brushing over, or a fly walking on your head, will be felt, across the face or hands. Often a cool breeze will blow. Throbs will be felt from within. Speak to the intelligence. Be friendly, sympathetic, loving and so invite and attract the spirit or spirits.

• • •

2

The Normal Sense And Organ Of Hearing

Scientists claim that the range of sound waves or vibrations which the sense of hearing can apprehend and comprehend are from 40 to 40,000 per second.[1] Etherial radiation is much higher, quicker and yet it is neither perceptible to the sense of sight, hearing or any other normal sense. If light waves travel at the rate of 400 to 700 billions per second and the eye can catch them, and not the vibrations called ethereal waves, emitted by electrical oscillation, one would quite naturally suppose that auditory vibrations are much lower in scale than either optical or ethereal. And there is ground for concluding that most persons are more inductive to sound than to light waves. But how about the clairaudient perception or the electrical or etheric ear, to use a similar phrase which Lord Kelvin employed when speaking of the "Electric eye?"

Sir Oliver Lodge seems to believe that between the highest audible, and the lowest visible vibrations there has been hitherto a great gap which these electric oscillations go far to fill up.

But are the so-called "voices", "thoughts", "spirit language", waves with which any material instrument, however delicate, can deal? Does clairaudience or clairvoyance deal with vibrations which occupy this hitherto unknown gap? And if so does this clairaudient (supernormal) perception imply an etheric, supernormal organ, function or sense which apprehends and then translates to the spirit through the so-called etheric double made up of finer matter, or spiritual body as Paul called it, these inaudible sound waves? This is possible, and yet as thought does not depend upon, nor is it created by sensation, although

. it is intelligently related to it, so spirit language can be spoken as between excarnate and incarnate spirits without organic functions. Confusion and misunderstanding arise when the normal (mental) habit or mode of seeing and hearing are theoretically made the universal (supernormal), interior, as well as exterior, means of intelligent communion and communication.

Nor will a specification of the organization, office and integral parts of the function of the ear help us to understand the sense of hearing, or spiritual hearing. The ear, the organ and the sense are physically adapted to sound waves and are marvellously composed. And yet spirit speaks and can speak to the spirit without them. Some one will ask, "Why then this apparent waste and extravagance on the part of nature!" There is neither waste, nor extravagance but economic provision and wise necessity in the organic and functional arrangement. While material but partial knowledge is as necessary as spiritual and complete knowledge, and while one opens the door of the spirit to the outer kingdom so that the man finds Divinity in his humanity, the other opens the door to the inner kingdom, and finds Divinity to be all in all. Who then will deny the disadvantage but necessity of experience through the normal senses and mind, but the advantage and freedom of life through the supernormal senses and consciousness?

The efficiency or inefficiency of the sense of hearing (deafness), affects the clairaudient hearing only, as the mind is unfamiliar with the objective images and language of thought, and among such cases where materiality of thought predominates. Thought to the spirit is the inspiration of intelligence, while language, symbolical as it is, is but one of its forms of expression. But inasmuch as it is through language that the mind of man perceives and understands thought as it relates to material things, everything having a name, so the spirit people feel obliged to relate their thought and even inspirations to the symbols, forms, idioms of our mental world, which we associate with ideas. This will more and more become apparent as the law of the subjective in relation to the objective mind is revealed and intelligently understood. So, if spirit people address mortals clairaudiently, as spirit to spirit, their inspirations, thoughts and ideas commonly fit into the moulds or forms by and through which we breath or associate our own ideas.

There is a purer language, a more chase form of communion, than the shadows of our thought forms which constitute the media of all spirit communion by clairaudience; but as the life and thought of the spirit people must be expressed by the law of dissimilitude, and though that law corresponds with the life and thought of mortals, still mortals, except in rare and exceptional cases, as among extremely pious and saintly men and women, cannot comprehend the higher forms or modes of thought radiation, spiritual or divine inspiration. And so while the objective will overshadow the subjective, and the subjective will overshadow the spiritual, spiritual things, as Paul wrote, must indeed be spiritually heard as well as discerned. And this basic fact of the operations of the spirit, oscillating, as it were, between the two hemispheres of the one world, the human and divine, the material and spiritual, is important to recognize in our mental attitude, both to spirit people and the spirit, or we shall not understand exactly the science of clairaudient communication and communion.

EXPERIMENT 2

As you sit quietly resting the body as you relax the mind, gradually enter the subjective sphere of the mind. This can be attained by prayer, concentration and meditation. This is not a half-hearted, perfunctory, academic exercise, but a joyous, sympathetic, intelligent service, full of faith and trust; for remember that "faith is the substance of things hoped for", but a subjective and spiritual substance, so compelling and inspiring in its sublime, spiritual quality as to actually become "the evidence of things unseen." The substance is in reality what you are aspiring for,—not what you are in the objective mind or body. As you listen and familiarize yourself with this virgin or occult, subjective sphere, soon evidences of spirit presence will be realized. A voice,—a word or sentence,— perchance only an impression,—a thought, or a feeling, will startle you with its thrill and inspiration. It will prove that it proceeds from within,— where you are now thinking,—from the spirit. Talk to it, and let it join in your meditations. It will reveal its identity to you sooner or later, but do not doubt it, nor grieve it. Sympathy, and not antipathy is the safe, sound and reliable law of spirit communion.

• • •

3

Sound Vibrations And Ether Waves

Clairaudience as a supernormal function has to do with ether waves only in so far as the ethereal body of the spirit relates itself to sound vibrations. A vibration which produces a sound is very much lower in the scale of vibrations than ether waves. But as ether waves convey, include and define higher, even spiritual rates of vibrations, it is not at all unthinkable to surmise, if not to advance as a fact of psycho-chemistry and psychophysics, that in some mysterious way not yet intelligible to the physicist or psychologist, what an excarnate spirit wills, thinks or feels is, to use a normal word, "sensibly" impressed upon the ethereal body or organism of the recipient on the physical plane, so that he feels, sees, or hears the thought as the case might be, or as the operator chooses to transmit it. Sometimes the thought is better felt than seen, at other times it is better heard than either felt or seen. And so the employment of these sublime forms of vibrations which offer no resistance to thought, and which seem to bridge the hiatus between the planes of the incarnate and excarnate spirits.

It is not here declared that ether waves are necessary to deductive thought or inspirational transmissions; but it is maintained that where spiritual (inner) communion is not possible or practical, thought waves act upon and through ether waves to set up correspondential and lower waves by which intelligent messages are transmitted by what may here be called the cypher code, to minds keyed to lower and not to higher vibrations. This must and will be self-evident to any one who will give the relationship between the sense world and sound waves in which man finds himself organically fitted, and the spirit world and ether waves in which the spirits functioning on the supernormal and excarnate planes find themselves adapted. For instance, I may think your thought without you being conscious of the fact, and I may tell you to your surprise, but when you must speak or write the thought, you employ material means and the voice conveys to me by sound waves, as the letters conveys to me by waves of light your thought. Could we commune in thought alone we need employ no sound or light waves. So, in the use of the supernormal power of clairaudience. When Spirit communes with spirit, ether waves which vocalize to the ethereal organism the thoughts of the spirit, are necessary. And this conception of an organic correspondence between spirits in the atmospherean and etherian worlds show that where the souls of men have not outgrown their earthly and sense attractions some wise organic or functional provision is made for them.

This idea or fact of planes, however actual on the physical and real or ethereal on the superphysical side of human life, must not be made too material or literal, or one will imagine that the air or ether as the case might be, are necessary to an intelligent perception or consciousness of thought. On the contrary spirit incarnate or excarnate only need functions, so long as they fail to enjoy life without them. Atrophy will set in the moment the spirit ceases to use an organ. Regeneration of the organ as well as the life that uses it must first take place.

The "third" eye of Theosophists is not another eye added to the two which man now uses, but one eye, the spirit's own sight, and as .a matter of fact no eye at all, which needs an organic outlet or holes in the skull to make vision possible, as clairvoyance proves. So it is with the "third" ear—the sense of hearing, which is clairaudience, and which hears without an ear and is spiritual.

Thus "I" hear sound waves, or "I" hear ether waves which are a superlative excitation of the ether by supernormal spirit vibrations; but to hear spiritually, the "I" hears directly spirit, with spirit, a hearing more contiguous, and interior than sense hearing, because within one's own consciousness. When two spirits commune thus, one the recipient and the other the percipient, what inspirational possibilities spread before them!

EXPERIMENT 3

The psychological test which is extremely helpful in deducing this clairaudient experience is one which is employed when the soul is in trouble. It goes within itself to find a way out of itself,—that is, out of the difficulty. Rely less and less upon audible advice and more and more upon inaudible. Listen for and to the vox dei or the voice of God, and, in so listening, other voices will speak out of the silence, within your own consciousness and take up the threads of thought just where we are thinking. Do not expect any superlative revelation in thunderous tones of the "Thus saith the Lord." Listen day by day, and love to listen, for the voices of the spirits, and the voices of the spirit will sooner or later respond to your prayer or cry for help. As egotism destroys the possibility of inspiration, one must lay the thought of self-sufficiency, as well as selfishness, at the door before entering the silence. Let what you seek be good for you and for all, then sure results will follow. This is a safeguard against the evils of auto-suggestion, and the greater evils of self-hypnosis and obsession.

• • •

4

The Silence

A great deal has been written and said about the silence, and most students of the new psychology and occult science have an intelligent if not a clearly defined conception of what the silence means. And yet it has been often defined in terms so misleading and ambiguous that we know what it is most by what it is not. It is within the mind, and yet it is neither a form, nor a product of thought. It is not the subjective in contradistinction to the objective mind. It is not a mental pose or attitude, although relaxation or passivity of the mind is necessary to realize it. It is not thoughtlessness, nor thoughtfulness, although the silence is that state of mind, which neither the absence nor the presence of thought can define. Mental unconsciousness, called the trance, is not the silence, and yet it often sweeps one into it and gives ecstatic and supernormal experiences. Absent mindedness or distraction as in oblivion and reverie is not technically the silence, for they imply conditions imposed on consciousness rather than that sublime, rarified state designated the silence.

Mental scientists have treated the silence as though it were the subjective reservoir, from which one draws positive response to all objective suggestions while metaphysicians, the spiritual or divine scientist treat it as the oracle of prayer or aspiration, the Holy of Holies, which mediates the ego between the outer (objective mind) and inner court (subjective mind) of intelligence and God.

Excellent and splendid as are these suggestions on the subject of the silence, that of the divine scientist approaches nearest to our own definition of it. Mental action and inaction, thoughtlessness and thoughtfulness, interior and exterior methods of inducing stillness are supplimentary and auxiliary to the state itself which the silence defines. It is a spiritual before it is a mental state of passivity or physical condition of rest. And the word spiritual implies and explains more than, and all that the other words vaguely convey.

A spiritual state is a permanent quality or capacity of consciousness, which no sense perception or experience can define or make clear. It is the spirit's own possession which the pure character or life alone will reveal and make a source of power, plenty and peace. It is the well of living water within each one, so truly and symbolically described by John in the Fourth Chapter of his gospel, of which every outward, full or stagnant well of water, (the mind) is but a gross caricature or coarse dissimilitude. For the life that is running away from us in the adulteries of thought and action, as in all that leads the soul to lose itself in the world of pleasure, makes a farce of the silence, and until the awakening comes, as in the prodigal son, the soul will not know rest or peace, until it finds them within and above, whence they come.

To be still is the one crying need or condition of the physical man or woman; but it is not enough or all; for to realize that which is within the mind, after the storm of worry has abated and the sky of mind has cleared, and the cost or loss is known, one must be willing and ready to live the spiritual life which qualifies one to understand and realize the silence. This is why many "brands" and "substitutes" which are offered as "just as good" and which are accepted as genuine, prove valueless. "Narrow is the way which leads to life," and few indeed love it sufficiently to seek life on the only way where it can be found, but prefer the broad way of humbugs and brands, which counterfeit the spiritual. Yet the silence alone is found on "the narrow way" and strange to say, it is begun in this life just where one is in thought and action. The scriptural broad way is not a way at all, in the strict use of the word, but the experience of the senses, while the narrow way is the realization of one's Divinity.

A text book of the new psychology which deals with the language, powers and life of the spirit must borrow from Divine or mystical science adequate and comprehensive definitions of these words. For

Divine or Mystic science is supersensuous and spiritual, rather than sensuous and intellectual in its revealments, and it treats of spirit, the spiritual life and the spiritual world as such, and from the consciousness and realization of them, and not theoretically or dogmatically, nor from the intellectual view point. Hence, the silence can never be obtained by any intellectual, or moral process, or by intellectual or moral culture, refined as it may be, but is and must be a spiritual attainment. This does not mean that physical, intellectual, and moral rules for obtaining external stillness, harmony of mind and beauty of surroundings should be ignored; but it means that the stillness, harmony, aesthetical alone, can never take the place of, or be substituted for the state of the spirit, in which the silence lies potentially as "the treasure hidden in the field." Many intellectually trained minds may scoff at this statement, as the Pharisees of old who ridiculed many of the mysteries of the spirit which Jesus Christ taught. But to those who aspire for Reality, and are not satisfied with reflections, who prefer sunlight to moonlight, the word initiation will mean as much as regeneration, and they will open and close two doors,—as they pray and purify themselves, one, the physical and the sensuous, the other, the mental and the ethical,—and take the third degree of perfection by entering the shrine or Holy of Holies of the spirit.

Lest some may think such language too ambiguous to be practical, they need only to be reminded that the purest and best in this life and the life which is to come is not an intellectual (mental), nor a material, but a spiritual possession, and as such is the supreme necessity. Useful as a material body is to the spirit, it is discarded when death calls the spirit to another life and world. All that that body attracted or described by its environment, and earthly possessions, remain on earth or perishes with it. The mind, which is the finer objective body, or tool of the spirit, no less serviceable and valuable, disintegrates as a vapor, and though capable of being reproduced in vitascopic memory by the spirit, is as perishable as the body. The intelligent ego that used the body and the mind slips behind the scenes when the curtain falls, to become better acquainted with itself, after the masquerade of form, paint, tinsel and action have been removed.

What has the spirit thus denuded of a physical body done to qualify itself for the higher condition, the inner state of its post-mortem existence? Did it lock the doors of the senses, to express and realize the supernormal powers, so that in consciousness here and now it could feel, hear, see, think and act divinely, and not as one in slavish captivity or obsessed by the senses? Did it shut out terrestrial sights to see visions celestial? Did it shut out earthly sounds and voices, to hear heavenly music and the voices of the silence? Not that it should hate, spurn and abhor all outward things, but rather augment the human with the divine, that it should not allow the sensuous to have dominion over it, drawing it away from the sphere of freedom, truth, love, peace and bliss.

For no one can either enter or abide in the silence whose senses are actively engaged, and are not closed to worldly pleasures; nor can any one hope to function sanely on the supernormal plane who, at any time, allows the allurements of outward senses to absorb him. This is all important.

If the silence were received by entering some outward tabernacle and there becoming worshipful, instead of betaking one's self to an inner shrine, and there proving one's worthiness; if it were more a condition of the mind, and less a state of life and consciousness, it would be easily obtainable. But ingress to the spiritual world of realities is no less a path inward toward God, as it is an abnegation of the very influences and things which obstruct that blessed and luminous path, and compels a sacrifice of self, and a working, humanitarian love of mankind. So that while there is both a superphysical and psychological side of the silence, which to some is its most important side, because technically and most easily comprehended, the spiritual, ethical and practical side, which to the mass of students is neglected or slighted, is the key to the revealments of the silence itself. Theory, however excellent and practical is not here misprized, but it is applied with absolute fidelity to deduce results. For the silence is not a reception room where outward conversation ceases and no inward communion takes place, but it is the meeting place of the soul with all over souls, of spirit with spirit, the lover with the beloved in the deep divine sense. And here the broken hearted, the comfortless, the bereaved,—all who yearn for the "touch of a vanished hand, and the sound of a voice that is still," can receive direct evidences from their spirit loved ones, who draw nearer them in the silence, in love and devotion.

Mysticism is the science of the silence; it means exactly what the silence defines. For the mystic is one who knows how to seal lips, eyes and ears, that he may consciously enjoy the arcana of the spirit and the spiritual world, the communion of spirits. And thus a spirit can, and does commune with spirit as his own inner experiences prove.

To the eastern or western occultist the silence is the inner oasis where the weary pilgrim stops for a time to drink deeply of its crystal waters before pushing on to paradise. As such, it lies, as it were, midway between the subjective and spiritual sphere of the soul, and that sphere is the human consciousness.[2]

The soul is as active when in the silence as it is passive before it enters it, but such activity is supermental as well as supersensuous, and, therefore, it can best be defined by the compound subjective or spiritual communion. To subjectify one's self is not necessary to withdraw from the sense world, although one does consciously withdraw from the objective physical life. But to spiritualize the subjective mind is to allow the consciousness, free of mental or sensuous activity, to declare itself, and so unite, blend, or fuse with spiritual realities.

This is how the silence becomes a means of percipiency and recipiency, so far as telepathic and clairaudient communications are concerned. The percipient sends or posts his messages as the recipient receives them in the silence, and to the extent that both the percipient and recipient consciously realize, telepathically, the office and value of the silence and so enter it,—they are able to successfully transmit and receive clairaudient and telepathic messages.

Fundamental conditions must be complied with before results can be expected, and the wise student is one who will not neglect necessary, although not always accepted rules for the attainment of the silence.

EXPERIMENT 4

Realize at each sitting that the silence is obtained best by listening inwardly, or spiritually. By so directing the attention the ego will polarize the mind on this form of service, and so enable the spirit friends, who are seeking to reach and help you, to clear the way for clairaudient rapport and communion. Listen! The voices of the silence are soundless, but not speechless. They manifest intelligence and love.

• • •

5

The Objective And The Subjective Mind As The Spectrum Of Sound Waves And Clairaudience

Clairaudience is the apprehension, perception and the realization of the spirit of all sounds. As sound travels in waves and these wave lengths differentiate and define sounds, the message is intelligible and never audible to the spirit. Sound never touches the spirit, but the spirit of sound does. The objective and subjective minds act as sounding boards, reflecting sound waves and are, in fact, spectra by which sounds translate their message into their integral parts where articulate language builds its variety of alphabets, which are letters designating certain vowel or consonant forms of composite sounds,. The spoken word preceded all uttered or written speech. John, the mystic, wrote that "In the beginning was the word, and the word was with God, and the word was God." So that the "word" composed of two consonants and two vowels becomes when truly interpreted, the exact word of God, key to the symbolic square of the Jewish tabernacle, I. H. V. H., which in Hebrew stands for "Jehoveh," and is unpronounceable, Adonai being substituted for it.

The name of God is numerically, cabalistically equal to 26, or the word. The vowel O as a symbol in the word "word" stands for spirit,—so that the breath (spirit) lies back of or within the waves which manifest it. What the spirit knows it manifests through sounds expressed in vowels and consonants. Granted, that when spirit first uttered or manifested a sound, the "word" was there inspiring it, and that the spirit could not utter a sound without law and that law was the will of God, and that the word was God. It is evident that form, life and spirit, or matter, soul and spirit, are words which will intelligently define what the office or function of the word was. And when such language is expressed scientifically as well as Biblically, the power of spirit is shown in the fact that matter has its key note which determines its plane of manifestation.

The objective mind breaks sound waves up into their sense forms which become intelligible to the spirit, functioning outwardly through the sense world; while the subjective mind, which deals in part with these forms as thoughts, breaks them up into forms of ideas which become intelligible to the spirit, functioning inwardly through the supersensuous world. A simple illustration will make this clear. Take John's mystical "word" for example. The word in the world of matter may be a chair, a house, a horse,—and the spirit forms an image or thought of the object in the objective mind; but when the spirit relates it to the subjective mind, the concrete chair, house or horse, becomes an idea, which is the basis of any number or kind of chairs, houses or horses; so that if a clairaudient is communing with a spirit, a particular chair, house or horse could be cited exactly corresponding with the one seen, or the subject could be mentioned and discussed with a concrete, sense, conception of what is meant.

This is the mode of inspiration from the spirit world to the mind of mortal; from an interior sphere within the spirit to an exterior plane apparently outside mind. Now reverse the mode. How can a mortal apprehend, think of or realize the imagery, realities or similitudes which make up or belong to the distinctly spirit and spiritual world, the abode of immortals? If earth's language, idioms and forms of speech, describe the mortal's conception of material objects, how can these same conceptions, gross or fine, possibly define the immaterial, superphysical and supersensuous? Even if by the law of correspondence a vague sense of the dissimilitude between material, or sense, and spiritual perception of outer and inner things can be had, still man must consciously function as a spirit disembodied in the spirit or spiritual world, to be able to know the difference. And then the spiritual experience will be lost or fade into opposite likeness when he awakens to the sphere of secondary or self consciousness.[3] And in this conditioned consciousness, or mind, his visions often become only dreams or reminiscences, or shadow forms of realities which are too supermental to be expressed in forms of sensuous experiences.

Primary consciousness is that which deals with spirit as it is, the spirit world and life; the secondary, with subjective and objective mind.

Inasmuch as the subjective mind, and not the objective, or representative mind, is creative, it is called subjective and lies closer to the spirit, embracing it. Consequently, to become a clairaudient one must learn to occupy it and live in it, and this can only be done, first technically, by psychologically watching the process of the formation or generation of one's thoughts; secondly by morally and spiritually purifying these same thoughts and keeping the mind clear and pure; and finally, by spiritual introspection and meditation. All this is not a perfunctory, but a glad, willing, service.

Now some students imagine that the words objective and subjective refer to two different kinds of mind, whereas they refer to one mind, under two different conditions. Remove the condition called objective and subjective, and mind remains, but remove the condition called subjective, and the objective appears. Remove both the objective and subjective conditions and the mind ceases to become or be a mind. It is not unconsciousness but consciousness. It is consciousness that makes "mind" possible. It is the polarization of the consciousness upon object, the sense concept or percept, a material thing—or subject, the idea which gives to objective and subjective minds their distinct differences and definitions. Many suppose that the subjective mind is wholly latent, occult, potential, that subconscious sphere of the soul's life which is not yet brought to the surface of self, or active consciousness, whereas it is active in its passivity, as any practical, new or old, school psychologist knows who treats with it suggestively. On the same ground spirit might be said to be non-existent because psychology only deals with objective, rather than subjective or hyper-subjective states or conditions of the mind.

Clairaudiently the spirit is functioning only through, or by means of the subjective mind, because the subjective is a deeper, less sensuous, more ideal mind. For when the mind becomes objective it deals with coarser mind stuff or matter, grosser substances of thought which are impossible to the subjective. Now, if one applies the word "spiritual" to mind, or to thought, whether the mind or thought be objective or subjective, the mind or thought is at once conceived of as free of either the objective or subjective condition and limitation, and this is the nature of the life of the spirit, called the divine life, which no other form of life can express; and its experiences are those of the spirit and not of the senses.

The supernormal senses deal with the supernormal life and world, called, also, supersentient, because above and beyond the limited sphere of the normal, five senses; but these senses can be adulterated as grossly as can the physical. But because supernormal they cover the range of experiences which are not sensuous. However, the subjective mind, and the sphere of the active supernormal powers as clairvoyance, clairsentience and clairaudience, seem to be one and the same, and yet nothing is farther from the truth. With the supernormal powers one can pierce the veil of flesh, penetrate the subjective mind and function on the astral or ethereal planes, where the excarnate spirits function and live. But to the extent that one is spiritual will the use of normal or supernormal powers be sane, wise and beneficial. Otherwise, there is grave danger from certain forms of obsessions. This is mentioned not to inspire fear, but as a warning, because some novitiates who dare to express supernormal powers are not always ready or willing to live a pure life; and so when chaos, darkness, madness follow their futile efforts to take the spirit world by violence, the public should blame and condemn them and not the masters, teachers or guides whose instruction and example these psychic adventurers and filibusters defiantly ignored.

The mind as the spectrum of thought as evidenced in experience yet serves the spirit in the supernormal, clairaudient sense. And excarnate spirits who seek audience with those to whom they are attached, often use, in fact, generally employ the same idioms and forms of speech to make their thought intelligible. And this is not strange or unnatural.

It would be strange and unnatural were their thought not manifest to those on earth as it is. How could any one on earth interpret thought as a force or a wave, or a vibration, if it did not, as the comb or cylinder of a music box respond with a tone which became an integral note of a beautiful melody? There are no new notes; there are no new letters; but notes can be arranged to create new tunes; so letters can form words expressing new ideas. Psychologists in dealing with clairaudient phenomena must not expect a new language, nor a new order of thought which the average mind of man cannot comprehend; but he should expect in the deeper, sublimer, clairaudient perception such imagery as befits the soul of a vision, or the spirit of a heavenly voice. But this will not be until the mind of man is purified or spiritualized and so prepared for such transcendent inspiration.

Spirits in clairaudient communication with mortals must employ thought, and it is the office of the subjective and objective mind to embody the thought in intelligent form; whether the thought be relative to the life of the spirit excarnate or incarnate it must be made intelligible, and this is why the mind acts as a spectrum.

EXPERIMENT 5

Observe how impressions and inspirations arise in the mind. Do this not when passive or active, but whenever these impressions or inspirations arise, and in this way a clearer perception and a deeper understanding will be had of how clairaudient communication becomes possible.

• • •

6

Thought In Relation To Sound, And Inspiration In Relation To Clairaudient Speech

Sounds are descriptive, audible cyphers of thought, unintelligible until the code is revealed or explained. In them the spoken thought for the fleeting moment lives. Sounds reflect the voice in the voices, for the voice is the distinctive oracle of sound waves. As there are seven notes, each one manifesting a certain sound in the musical scale, and each sound canonically representing the interval between the planets as measured by the tone which is the distance of the moon from the earth, so this scale of seven notes expressing the music or harmony of the spheres, finds an exoteric meaning in the seven vowels which may be called the seven out-breathings of the soul.

Philology teaches that all sounds, so far as the alphabet or letters are concerned, are syllables, composite rather than elemental. As there are five general vowels (A. E. I. O. U.) which represent the five senses, they are assigned integrally and essentially to certain members of the human organism, and of the head in particular. Thus hieroglyphically they relate to certain parts of the building known in esoteric masonry as Solomon's Temple. All this can be more fully elaborated under ideography which graphically analizes the organic and functional senses, assigning to the ears—hearing, to eyes—seeing, to nose—smelling, to tongue—tasting, and to mouth or lips—touch.

Each organ except the tongue, is dual. As the hands are two and are composed of five fingers, they are said to be the foundation of gesture language. The idea prevails that two or duality are but complements of one, while the number ten, as in the five fingers of each hand suggests

 CLAIRAUDIENCE

that the exoteric and esoteric senses are five each. The sense of touch is as much in the hands as in each of the five specialized organs as each sense is a function of feeling. So much for vehicles.

Speech is intelligence expressed in sounds. Therefore, however elemental or complex speech may be, however infinite and differentiated the original and simple means of the earliest vocal utterance or communication may have been, thought to be intelligible from the standpoint of spirit must appeal to the human mind through thought forms. If the words "transcendental" and "immanent" were applied to the word speech, such words would give speech a higher and an inner meaning, which the word "uttered" or "spoken" could not do. Speech need not be spoken, and if transcendental or immanent, as the sentence "Thus saith the Lord" must be conceived, it is heard clairaudiently, spirit by spirit; and not as though addressed outwardly by vocal sounds to the normal sense of hearing. This does not mean, nor imply that to hear clairaudiently one may not hear sounds as though supernormally spoken. For sound is after all but an appearance or body of thought, appealing to the sense of hearing, as a vision is but an appearance or body of thought appealing to the sense of seeing. And a psychic or subjective sound may be heard as loudly as a physical sound or an objective sound. But clairaudient communication as a rule, and as differing from normal hearing, is not dynamic but soundless. Therefore, the use of the words higher or transcendent and inner or immanent forms of speech.

No doubt the word "inspiration" will throw some light on this seemingly mysterious process. Take a concrete example. A spirit wishes to talk with a mortal. If the mortal is highly sensitized and realizes in his or her atmosphere the influence of spirits, he is all attention. He listens. He may think of or speak inaudibly to the familiar and beloved spirit friend or helper. If he hears clairaudiently, what he hears will often (not always) enter into the immediate thought which is present as the inspiration of the moment. Let this following conversation, now make this clear. His thought or inspiration,—"Dearest, (his wife) is here?" The spirit: "Yes, it is your Dearest."

Did you rest well last night?" he asks. "Yes," she replies, "I rested very well." "Spirits do not sleep," she adds. Then she asks, "Are you going out for a walk?" He answers, "Yes, Dearest, presently." Now, were the conversation to be less social and intimate, or more intellectual and spiritual, the same colloquial form would be used and the inspiration might be something of this nature, which takes place while they are on the walk. He passes a lonely road running along a cemetery. The inspiration leads him to think of how foolish it is for so many Christians to imagine or believe that when they lay away the dead body in the tomb or grave the spirit sleeps with it until doomsday or the alleged day of the judgment. To this thought which arises in his mind the spirit speaks clairaudiently. "Isn't it too bad that so many imagine that their spirit friends are with their bodies in the graves, instead of with their loved ones as spirits in their earthly homes?" "Yes," he replies, "superstition born of ignorance is not yet dead." The words, idioms of speech, language belong to the mortal mind. The spirit inspires the mortal to think thoughts conjointly with mortals, expressing them colloquially in a language, most often that of the clairaudient, nevertheless substantially what the spirit thinks now or would think were it actually on earth in a physical form.

Inspiration is not always unique or original, yet in the common affairs of life it is spiritually useful and helpful, because always making mankind realize his Divinity, and that his true guidance is from within and above. Students who are not consciously inspired, and others who connect inspiration with some external source, and still others who believe that it wells up from within the spheres of one's own consciousness, often form extremely grotesque and abnormal conceptions of what inspiration really is. The theological doctrine of plenary inspiration has done a great deal to vitiate and depreciate such inspiration as is our common heritage from the spirit world, while it has doctrinally taught that divine inspiration is either supernaturally impossible with most men, or a favor shown a few by a special act of the Divine will, which is absurd. Inspiration is as universal and as common as thought, as has elsewhere been shown,[4] and all ideas are rooted in and spring from it.

Paul, in referring to the gifts or powers of the spirit speaks of the "the voices," and in several chapters of Corinthians shows that, as was the common practice in the Church among the early Christians many spoke in unknown tongues. He insisted that the clairaudient medium should see to it that the message was explained or translated by an interpreter. Otherwise, the voices were unprofitable. Some were mediums for Greek, Syrian, Jewish, and, no doubt, ancient spirits who spoke in their own vernacular. Only those who were familiar with these different tongues or languages could intelligently receive or comprehend what was said. Hence he advised an interpreter to be on hand when these influences appeared or obsessions occurred. It is not unlikely that a Syrian could be, or was controlled by a Greek, and a Greek by a Hebrew,—few mediums today have received such tests, but this must not be forgotten or overlooked,—that in the company of the Christians among whom these demonstrations of the spirit became possible, there were those who spoke these tongues. However, the Greek spirits could not edify the Hebrew mortals, by speaking in a language they could not comprehend, but they could enlighten them if they inspired them to think in their own tongues or to think at all. And this is the lesson which is here taught. Thought is languageless in the spirit world and only manifests in the moulds of language, numbers or symbols when spirits express thought to mortals.

It is a law that whatever modes or forms of knowledge prevail, so far as they manifest thought, these become the vehicles of inspiration through which ideas and revelations are conveyed. And as these modes or forms change or become useless, other forms or modes being substituted for them in the natural and spiritual order of the soul's life, so the inspirations of the spirit world use them. As Jesus said, referring to this fact, no one puts new wine into old bottles.

So in clairaudient discourse with mortals, the spirit world thinks as we think, thinks its thoughts into our present forms of speech, and inspires our intelligent understanding, and when the thought is newer or higher than we have known, it conveys it to us often by coining new words, or using sacred rather than vulgar words, that is, words which are radically simple and spiritual and are not subject to jugglery or ambiguity.

To hear spiritually one must more and more be spiritual in thought and life.

EXPERIMENT 6

Try to listen and hear the thought of a spirit by asking a question which involves less and less of knowledge of material things, but more and more a knowledge of spiritual. Realize that the answer may come first as an insensible breath or whispering, like a thought in substance and entering the mind as softly. Continue to apply this method, and continue to listen. Better keep a diary of your impressions or experiences. In an incredibly short time there will be given unmistakable evidences of spirit presence and conversation.

● ● ●

7

The Law Of Correspondence Clairaudiently Applied

Since Swedenborg's death the law of correspondence has been given a wide and an ever widening definition. It is not so much a law of similitudes as dissimilitudes; things which are alike resemble each other on outer and inner planes in appearance only. And, therefore, the natural and spiritual body differs not in identity but in substance and representation. The spirit operating on the spiritual planes uses and needs no organ called a brain, with which to think, nor functions called eyes and ears, with which to see and hear, and yet it thinks and sees and hears, but not as these operations of the organic man are understood. So that unless the law of correspondence be spiritually as well as organically understood, one will be led to suggest or imagine that the new functions are but the old organs, with their physical appurtenances etherialized. No fancy is more fanciful and no suggestion is more erroneous.

An old teaching declares that "all things in the heavens exist on earth in an earthly form, and all things on the earth exist in the heavens in a heavenly form."

The law of correspondence does not imply similar nor dissimilar organs or functions of seeing or hearing, but higher modes of perception. And since flesh and blood do not obtain in the spirit, or spiritual world, the powers of the spirit need no longer organs or senses which relate to corporeal things. When, therefore, the pineal gland or organ of the third eye (clairvoyant sight which is supposed, in some quarters, to be the seat of that clairvoyant power which in time, by radical unfoldment, will again appear and be organically and physiologically operative and catalogued, is substituted for the very limited but highly useful organs, the physical two eyes which mankind now uses, the correspondence between the physical and spiritual seeing is so gross and material on the one side, and so unnatural and unspiritual on the other that the law of correspondence is radically violated. Clairvoyance, or second sight, which should be called primary or first sight, because spirit is causal to matter, needs no material sense or organ, even when dealing with material objects, because that sight is psychic, supernormal and of the spirit, and is, in reality, the implied use of a free spiritual agency.

So, if one thinks of the spiritual correspondence of the sense of hearing, he will do well not to associate a material organ with clairaudience, which is a supernatural power of (spiritual) hearing, but rather a function which such hearing requires. And this function is hinted at, not only in all clairaudient communications, but in independent voices, which are heard, as it were, originating in the air, and in fact are voices of excarnate spirits made manifest and projected through the organs of speech of a medium, and so given a body or form of sound. That the so-called spiritual body is the astral or etheric body which is the potential possession of each one, but not commonly exercised or employed, is true, but the words spiritual, astral and etheric, have nice and recognized differences of meaning and uses in technical occult science which must be understood to be appreciated. The finer body of a spirit is in a constant state of flux; that fs, it is becoming active or remaining sluggishly dormant on its own plane, and is partaking of the fine or dense atmosphere or aura of the person. As one becomes spiritual, loving and expressing a spiritual life, so does the ethereal body appear stronger, more visible and more formative; for the soul using less and having less need of the grosser, physical organic body, and living, as well as functioning, more constantly in the ethereal body, refines the corporeal substance of the physical body, so that the power and glory of the finer ethereal body may actively appear, until the life discards the crude physical vestment altogether. Flesh, that is weight, disappears, complexion and eyes become clairfied, each sense is rendered more acute, old habits of life and attractions cease to annoy or abuse the conscience, while the inner man's spirit shines forth in ineffable brightness, under the alchemystical process. Death may and does sever the soul or spirit from a physical body, but it does not destroy the power of its attractions or attachments, and so death does not in the least disturb or alter the elemental and spiritual substance of the ethereal body.

Much of the deafness or lack of hearing begins in materiality of thought and life[5] before functional and organic defects appear. To clear the sense of hearing or the passage way of the spirit between the physical and spiritual (clairaudient) hearing, by spiritualizing the thought and life, is necessary before the harmonious correspondence can be had between the spirit in the ethereal and corporeal bodies. If it is true that as a man thinketh, so he is, how equally true is it that as a man lives, so he hears. And this fact is fully and solemnly declared by Jesus, when he spoke of those who, having eyes, saw not, and ears, heard not, what the spirit addressed to the spirit, clothed in a corporeal form. So that the correspondence between the corporeal and ethereal body, so far as the conscious expression of each supernormal (sense) power is concerned, must be effected, by the spirit in the life, before clairaudient mediumship, to say nothing of one's supernormal power of clairaudience, becomes a conscious realization.

Hearing spiritually is as important as seeing spiritually and both are often unfolded and realized synchronously. No one can raise the degree of expression or vibration of perception, without becoming at once aware in his own consciousness of superior, supernormal and spiritual clairvoyant and clairaudient experiences. And while technical rules can be and are offered as theorems of how to proceed in each experiment following the lessons, still no unfoldment and realization will be had until one conjoins theory with practice, and makes that theory and practice begin and end in a spiritual life.

It is said that mathematics is the law of right living, because there is only one truth. Yet figures and results may agree theoretically but will mean nothing except naught (0) raised to an infinite differentiation of zero,—that is abstraction, until realized as the supreme fact of life, the very law of spiritual living. Mathematics is but the scaffolding of another kind of process as exact in one's life. Certain things are done in order that they may be undone, wrote Mary E. Boole in "The ' Mathematical Psychology of Gratry and Boole." And again, "The true direction for progress is revealed to man at the moment when some thing which he has been constructing with elaborate care vanishes into nothing." So right thinking must lead to right living, as spiritual thinking to spiritual living, because the object of all living is life, as the end of all thinking is consciousness. And it is through the life as a process that the consciousness as the sphere of spirit will more abundantly appear in the ever deepening and unfolding of the life, through the finer modes and perceptions of the spirit. Seek more and more to make the corporeal one with the ethereal body by refining the latter and not degrading the former, through pure spiritual thinking, feeling and living, and the correspondence functionally will be obtained by which hearing will be spiritual and clairaudient as well as sensational or sentient. For clairaudience is a power within the present sentient power of hearing, awaiting all who are ready to express and realize it.

EXPERIMENT 7

Read Isa. Chapter, 29-18; 35-5; 42-18.

See New Testament, Mark 7-32.

• • •

8

Dependent And Independent Voices

In abnormal, supernormal and physical phenomena, which result from the action of spirits through mediumship and of one's own spirit functioning on the ethereal or astral plane, special attention must be paid to what are termed dependent and independent voices. Whether one hears clairaudiently, or hears dependent and independent voices, no voice of a spirit can reach a mortal except by means of the functions which make voices audible. This does not mean that spirits are so limited in the use of these functions or organs of speech and intelligence as mortals, but it does mean that they must reach us through these avenues. And this is the reason that messages are often grossly saturated and tainted with extraneous thought and organic conditions which change their quality or character, and often disqualify them as accurate and genuine transcripts of spirit communications. In the light of many new revealments of the laws of inspiration students of the new psychology will make allowance for these facts, and will not condemn or discard evidences which, however mixed they may be with extraneous matter, will yet be none the less valuable data on which to build a rationale of clairaudient communication. Now by dependent voices, we mean audient and clairaudient, which are classified under the head of normal and supernormal,—voices of speech which we make or hear by sound waves, and voices which though soundless are not speechless, but are heard within and clairaudiently as spirit hears spirit. By independent voices is meant the voices uttered through organism of a medium, but not voiced or spoken by the medium, and which are heard in the air near the head of the medium and seem to issue out of the lips and vocal organs of the medium without any effort on his part, though he may hear the voices and be conscious of the process. Some have condemned these voices as the result of fraud, alleging that the so-called medium is a ventriloquist. It is not at all strange nor unnatural that such a conclusion should be reached by the unenlightened and ignorant. Still it does not at all follow that such voices do not proceed from spirits plus the spirit of the medium. One's physical, material body seems extraneous to one's spirit, and is unspiritual, however, it is the manifestation of the spirit. It lies, as it were, as truly outside and on the periphery of the spirit, although dependent upon the life of the spirit, as a voice which floats out of a medium's throat and is heard in a bodiless or disconnected form in the air. This voice, however, could not be audible were it not connected by magnetic filaments of psychic force, to the vitality and nerve fluid of the medium and the intelligence of the excarnate spirit. Independent, it is and seems, so far as natural causation is concerned, but not in reality when spiritual causality uncovers principles of psycho chemistry, with which modern physical science is unfamiliar. And if one could understand how any form of intelligent life, having the faculty of uttering sounds, makes them, no one could doubt this seemingly bewildering phenomenon and greater mystery of the projection of the independent voice, by excarnate spirit power.

There is one fact, which to the deeper student of supernormal and mediumistic phenomena, has always seemed self-evident, and that is, that no science of life can be intelligible or complete until it rests its foundation as well as builds its superstructure on spirit; and since the object of Spiritualism as a revelation of the mysteries of life, is, to demonstrate this important fact, one can perceive why its claims are undeniable propositions, which in every generation, afforded proofs of their consistency and truthfulness. What is the new psychology but the revealment of the facts of the spirit in a higher form and light, thus showing that the loose and erroneous statements of a psychology established on physiology only is false, and is placing the pyramid of life on its apex. The whole system of education and thinking has suffered from this perversion of both the facts and principles of life; and it is not to be wondered at that the opposition to Spiritualism is still formidable, unfriendly and even sinister, not only among the educated classes but among the followers of institutional religion, who, while admitting the facts of the supernormal and spiritual life, yet sidetrack the main issue, and, like the ink fish, who spurts an inky fluid in the water about him, through which he escapes, so they take umbrage under a time-honored system of theology rotten to the core.

No fact of science or religion can be a fact which the spirit does not make true in life itself. When will this simple truth be understood and accepted?

Not every one can or will receive evidence of the independent voices, for not all are mediums for them; but when manifest, these voices can be traced to excarnate spirits, who, if proper conditions are offered, can afford proofs of their identity. And what is true of the independent is no less true of the dependent voices. It is spirit which speaks, whether audible or inaudible, whether by dependent (normal) or independent (abnormal) voices, to assure us that spirit can speak to spirit supernormally and spiritually.

EXPERIMENT 8

Study the relation and agreement between the ego and speech, between what it thinks and speaks. Observe in psychic and supernormal development how the same laws and conditions obtain. Read in the Bible references to the independent voices. Consult concordance under the head voice and voices.

● ● ●

9

Practical Methods For Clairaudient Development

In any treatise on the development of supernormal powers, whether these powers be designated intuitive or spiritual, or merely supermental, the practise of rules and principles which make these powers operative, is all important. When once the serious student realizes that his present physical senses have inlets to the spirit world as well as outlets to the world of phenomena, he then can patiently and diligently begin to apply himself to the task of bringing them to the surface of his self-consciousness, and of using and understanding them as superior sources of life, knowledge, power and inspiration. He learns, that like all things natural, they reveal themselves under certain conditions. If the ancient seers learned the secrets of supernormal and spiritual being by simplicity and abstemiousness of life, as was the case with Appolonius of Tyanna, the modern novitiates cannot afford to disobey the laws of the spirit. In fact, the stricter he adhers to or obeys the rules laid down by the masters, the fewer will be the obstacles he will have to encounter in his pathway. This cannot be too strongly insisted upon in the beginning. Sensitives do not fail because they are over patient or over-zealous. In spiritual unfoldment there are no tricks to learn, but there are disciplines to follow, and many physical weaknesses and mental habits to overcome. The path of initiation is indeed one of heaviness, toil and sorrow to all students who do not love self-sacrifice. However, if the student makes up his mind to seek and love the spiritual, transmutation becomes easy and soon passion dies, and the lower nature, once dominated by the five senses and their corresponding astral or psychic influences and environments, cease to annoy or to offer, either temptations or resistance. Then, the path inward to the shrine of the spirit will be one, not alone of silver and gold, but of joy and peace.

We shall now attempt to specify in detail the safest and sanest methods for interior realization or clairaudient expressions of spirit. Remember that spirit can, does and will commune with spirit both in the excarnate and incarnate form, and that communion will be super-physical or spiritual; therefore, in no sense phenomenal or noumenal, as these words are, in the technical language of occult science, understood. This fact cannot be too strongly emphasized. For many occult students expect spiritual communion to be a matter for physical eyes to see, physical ears to hear, and the normal faculties of the mind to perceive. This is the grossest misapprehension and error. To key the clairaudient sense to the supernormal octave, to use a musical term, is to refine the sense as well as spiritualize the life. No one can hope by formal concentration, or mere intellectuality, to realize in a practical way, either the fact that he is a spirit, or the fact that as a spirit, he can transcend the sphere of his normal five senses, express supernormal power and still be self-conscious. This is the prejudice, bom of ignorance, sustained and propagated by pedantic and scholastic theologians or materialistic philosophers and psychologists. And it is an error into which many students of psychology still fall who accept time-honored but false doctrines as better than actual personal knowledge of the soul itself.

1. In supernormal unfoldment, the trance is only serviceable as it deepens the ego's capacity and quality of consciousness; and while this may seem to be impossible, because to many the trance rather tends to extinguish, or at least to occult the self consciousness, the object of the trance is to reveal the higher and deeper planes and spheres of the soul's subjective and spiritual life. The so-called "dead' trance may mean that so far as physical perception and sensation are concerned the soul is temporarily cut off from them, and the bodily organism may be in a condition of catelepsy; yet the soul may be so free, so illumined in that condition, that could it in any human and

possible way, relate its superphysical experiences, the story it could tell would seem incredible. And exactly what such a soul accomplishes when liberated for the moment by the trance, the soul that mystically seeks its deepest spiritual self,—that self which it now objectifies and then subjectifies, but at last realizes by the divine, or pure, spiritual life,—realizes all this and more, step by step in consciousness. As sleep which locks the physical senses and so induces rest, dreams or visions, so the unconscious or conscious trance permits the ego to function in the suburbs of that deeper, higher self, which the ego can never know or realize when enthralled or obsessed by the five physical senses.

To enter this state is, broadly speaking, necessary to a superlative realization of the spirit. Reverie, day dreaming, prayer, meditation, solitude, the cultivation of the religious and spiritual life; dwelling in mountain clefts, or in higher places; the contemplation of the heavens, the reading and the study of such poetry as that of Mrs. Elizabeth Barrett and Robert Browning, and kindred authors; religious books, as the gospels; and above all the surrender of one's self to self sacrificing but loving service to the sick, poor, helpless, whoever and wherever they are. Of course, this takes the soul out of the cloister into the universe; out of self, into acts of love and human service to our fellowmen; out of the mere metaphysics and abstractions of life, into the active consciousness where the hemispheres of what man is and does unite to form the sphere of what man is, when the human part is sunk or absorbed in God.

Thus, the trance is the process by which the spirit passes over (to go across literally) from the objective, material, and sensuous, mental states and conditions of life, to the subjective, psychic and supernormal, spiritual life. And when this process becomes a regenerative as well as a transmutative process, the spiritual faculties express themselves Quickly and spontaneously. Spiritual death is a phrase which describes as no other phrase can, the active, material sensuous or unspiritual life. And nothing conduces to spiritual inertia and apathy more than worldliness and selfishness.

2. One's diet is all important. The simpler and more elemental the diet, the purer and more vegetarian the food, the better. Meat, condiments and stimulants of all kinds should be avoided. The appetites and desires should never be indulged or catered to at the expense of the spiritual life. Supernormal, and even normal sanity are attained best and quickest by the purest life and most spiritual diet. And since milk and eggs can be used, care should be taken that the system be nourished, but not impaired by a thoughtless and inadequate diet. Efficiency can best be obtained by a mixed vegetarian diet, but where the tendency is to acidity, foods which produce that result should, for the time, be discarded until the stomach recovers its normality and harmony. Spiritual development cannot obtain where organic inharmony prevails. And as it will take some time to clean the body of the filth, and to clear the mind of the habits of the sense world, in which the spirit has unconsciously degraded itself, persistent, watchful and patient effort will afford the quickest and most beneficent results.

3. Introspection is as important as meditation or concentration. Concentration is necessary to establish the will in the sphere where the life can best attain purity or spirituality. To form the habit of being spiritual is the best use of power as defined by "will." Then the senses can never obsess the will, nor lure it from unselfish service to mankind. Egotism and egoism as expressing self love and love of individuality and individualization will give place to altruism which is defined by the golden rule. That worship or service which finds and reveals God in good deeds, is a glory which pleases God the best, for it blesses both the doer and the doing.

Meditation is necessary as the soul aspires and grows; and as meditation concerns aspiration in the light of inspiration, truth descends as prayers ascend. Wisdom and understanding follow. Introspection and retrospection, are like the light and the shadow on the dial plate. One preceeds the other. Self examination should be crucial but never morbid nor wearisome. To always find fault with one's self, and never overcome weakness is to grow weak and hinder the soul's growth. Retrospection without an introspection which is prospective, that is, visional and optimistic, is like shutting one's eyes to the sunlight and all that it reveals. To think morbidly and grievously of past errors and sins, and never see light and blessedness ahead is to take a wholly unnatural, pessimistic and irrational view of life.

The object of introspection is not to find cause for judgment or blame, but for gratitude and thankfulness. For as one truly introspects, looks within, as the words mean, more and more will the way appear to a complete reconciliation if not a blending of the one true life in the two seeming opposite and opposing selves, the outer and lower, and the inner and higher self, which is, in reality, but the one self, functioning in this seemingly partitioned, incongruous and disharmonious manner. And where the means are used to tame the lion and make him as docile as the lamb, the Biblical story of Isaiah will not seem so impossible, even in one's own household where all sorts of beasts dwell, and not always peacefully together. The idea of Noah's ark, mystically interpreted is, that each sort of beast in opposites, that is, pairs, or twos, shall dwell where they can best carry out their work, without disarranging or destroying the unity and order of the colony that lives under the same roof. To have or to allow two opposing selves to live in the same house, is to invite disaster, but to make the lower, so called, do the work which only the lower can do, and is called upon to do, and the higher to inspire and guide the lower, is to understand the true meaning of service or discipleship in the sphere of master. There is altogether too much waste of time and energy on mere seeing and hearing, (sensationalism), while the subject of all this action is left unobserved and unfolded. Introspection is given a very high place in occult science. It begins where sensationalism ends and as it seeks to know the knower through the knowing, its inlook is more vital and important than its outlook. It turns the ego back upon itself, away from phenomena which enthrall it, to spirit which liberates and illumines it. And in clairaudient development introspection enables the soul to listen and hear as spirit speaks,—not in sound waves, but in thought and language addressed to the spirit from spirit.

EXPERIMENT 9

Learn more and more to introspect. Cease arguing. Learn to value truth above personal opinion or mere experience. Cultivate solitude and that habit of mind, which, when alone, seeks to find joy and solace in divine meditation and contemplation. Watch the soul and recall it from an inane and meaningless life to one of spiritual initiative. Listen for the Master. He is not far away. Listen! He will speak, only when you listen.

• • •

10

Sympathy And Antipathy. Concord And Discord. The Law Of Clairaudient Expression And Realization

A poet, under the divine afflatus, wrote that "Order is Heaven's first law." Surely chaos must result from discord as evil and error result from certain misapplied sympathies, and applied antipathies.

The use the soul makes of sympathy and antipathy establishes the morale of concord and discord. For sympathy and antipathy are more than organic, and temperamental likes and dislikes are sensational.

Sympathies are emotions which produce concords or harmonies, while antipathies produce their opposites, and the reason for this is obvious. Concords are made up of elements and forces which fuse or agree, and so integrate; while discords are made up of elements or forces, which, like water and fire, never mix without disintegration.

Mortal life is life so mixed with opposites as to perish in its effort to be.

Immortal life is the same life which is a unit of the spirit raised above terrestrial conflicts, and resurrected into the form which images deathlessness or Divinity.

Concord and order are spiritual attainments.

Our sympathies and antipathies have everything to do with normal and supernormal hearing, for the jarring or harmonious instrument, conditions the quality of vibrations. How true it is that many who teach harmony live lives of inharmony. Still harmony is the basis of musical sounds, the technique of musical science, is but a crude, natural mathematical law which manifests external rules or grammar;

but though the musical results of applied harmony are melodious and agreeable to the ear, and yet are composed of sharps and flats, spiritual harmony is essentially a divine state which material sounds can never express.

Sympathy is large among those who are naturally affectionate, but not so marked among those who are intellectual.

Antipathy is an opposing, but not necessarily hateful, sympathy. Sympathy is the soul of clairaudient communion or communication. Sympathy is positive, while antipathy is negative. One affords pure and high clairaudient expression; the other, impure and low. Sympathy and antipathy are not to be so defined as to always imply love on the one side and hate on the other, but rather attraction and repulsion. For if one loves his friend and hates his enemy, and allows himself to express such contradictions of spirit, his clairaudience will be marred, if not perverted. For such an one's feeling cannot be pure nor harmonious, and as a matter of fact he is destroying good by evil. Still one may be inspired in action by likes or dislikes which are instinctive or organic, that is, natural, and yet be able on the one hand, to receive (by virtue of the likes) and on the other to receive (by virtue of the dislikes) telepathic messages. For it is a well established fact of telepathists that where and when the sympathy between percipient and recipient is the strongest, the quickest and most accurate results are obtained.

In dealing with such apparent confusion of thought and work, as prevails in any community, as a result of the lives of the citizens, one would hardly believe that sympathy and antipathy could so affect persons as to make it possible for them to be at all in telepathic communication with each other. And where so many persons are selfish, absorbed in their own pleasures, one might conclude that the law here set forth would break down. But as a matter of fact among just such gross numbers the law expresses itself in a general way. Environment and desire, suggestion by an appeal from without from any source or cause whatever and susceptibility, are but the workings of sympathy and antipathy. And many who know nothing at all of such a law as telepathy, are nevertheless, unconsciously the victims, rather than the conscious operators of these occult forces so redundant in mankind. The evil and the good, so called, the criminal and respectable classes are amenable to this law. Impressions are given and received as naturally and consciously as electrical discharges are made and felt, although those who give or receive them are not always conscious of them. It is all a most subtile and subtle arrangement, in which the nicest and most mathematically accurate results follow. Experts in the new psychology know this occult resource and so apply themselves to understand and take advantage of it.

Sympathy is after all best explained by the word receptivity and antipathy by its opposite. For a sympathetic person is, as a rule, open and free to receive, while one who is dominated by antipathies locks the mind and heart against the intrusion of the influences of persons and things. Sympathetic persons succeed the most, antipathetic persons fail the most in telepathic experiments. Again, sympathetic persons invite and move in a sphere of concord, while persons of strong antipathies invite and move in a sphere of discord. This is especially true where sympathies and antipathies over balance each other, but not true where they are sufficiently poised. No individual can be all likes or dislikes, and, therefore, not all sympathies or antipathies; but let one or the other predominate or rule the will of the individual and telepathic results, such as we have described, will follow. Percipient and recipient can never hope to meet or operate harmoniously on cross lines of antipathy; and however much antipathy may be marked or strong in each one, unless they agree on sympathetic lines of thought or action, or objects which both like to admire, the results will be a failure. Contingencies often do arise which make even the expert wonder if the law has not been violated, but on closer inspection of the facts in the case, sympathy between percipient and recipient, the subject and object, brought the successful results.

Between spirits this is the law of the spheres—the miracle of association and inhabitation, the deeper meaning of the attraction and correspondence between the souls in lower and higher spheres. An aspiration invokes an inspiration, so the depth and the height, man and God meet spiritually. And in clairaudient communication and communion with (immortals) excarnate spirits, sympathy between parent and child, wife and husband, brother and sister, friend and friend, or the application of that new commandment of Jesus, "Love one another," which is the same as "Love your enemies" will go mighty far toward, and indeed cover the whole ground in obtaining the results.

No life fuses or unites with another by antipathy. It is sympathy that makes the whole world kin.

• • •

11

Invisible Helpers Who Adjust And Attune Clairaudient Nerves Or Psychic Wires. Operators Needed On The Excarnate Side

Anyone who is familiar with the mysteries of mediumship, a word, which by the medical profession is technically disposed of as a congenital derangement of the nervous system, and with the facts of supernatural psychology, knows that the spiritual hypothesis admits of unseen operators on the excarnate side of life, who are largely responsible for many abnormal and supernormal phenomena. In fact, what physicians suppose or allege is a congenital derangement of the nervous system, may in the end, prove to be the etheric body, pushing through or declaring itself as the original pro or antetype of the normal body on which the organic structure of atoms, cells, organs and system depend. As the physical form is a desire body, made so by generation, the etheric body is the definition of it, made so by regeneration. As the physical body embodies all that the desire body is, so the ethereal body reflects the shadow of the desire body as grossly or finely organized by the physical form. But the elasticity of the etheric or electrical body is made evident in mediums whose organism permits a rather free translation and correspondence between the active etheric and the active physical bodies. Abnormal phenomena are hints of supernormal powers, which belong to the ethereal body and are operative, in a natural way, in the grosser human organism. Without the finer etheric body, there is no grosser and the greater, freer powers of the one are the lesser, limited powers of the other. As spirits in the flesh can and do communicate with each other because spirit, so spirits disembodied do, under supernormal and abnormal conditions, communicate with each other. As mankind embodied learns the art of thus thinking, speaking, seeing and hearing, in fact, using all their normal powers, called faculties, senses, and organs, by education in the inspirational and intuitive, as well as experimental and tuitional sense, so supernormal help is bestowed by experts on the outer, physical (adepts) and inner, ethereal planes (discarnate masters). And it has! been found by the fearless and teachable scientist and psychologist, who has seriously studied Spiritualism, that Spiritualism in the broad and true sense, is (whatever it is not) the concrete effort of the spirit world to reach and teach mankind how to successfully communicate with their brethren in the spirit world, without shirking their present tasks or duties, or disqualifying themselves as sane, intelligent, human beings. No one wishes to be, or to be thought idiotic or insane, and one universal and fatal deterrent to the investigation and acceptance of Spiritualism, has been the fear or the superstition that it does lead to insanity; whereas the facts, or statistics as gathered from insane asylums, show that not one inmate in a thousand cases in such institutions were or are Spiritualists or ever investigated Spiritualism. Such libel originated among the ignorant and the foes of modern liberalism and truth.

To acknowledge, therefore, invisible helpers in the spirit world, who are seeking to reach humanity, is to place oneself in the receptive attitude to be helped. To follow sane, intelligent, spiritual advise which the guiding masters teach is to prevent dangers, either from obsessions, auto-suggestion, hallucinations, or vital drain, called vampirism, possible in rare instances among the illiterate and vicious who, like Glyndon in the story entitled Zanoni, "rush in where angels fear to tread," and who in short, expect results, without applying principles, and so end in insanity. Such would go insane if they never sought for abnormal or supernormal phenomena.

While it is true that one who uses the supernormal powers of clairsentience, clairvoyance and clairaudience can feel, see and hear spiritually, it follows that if there was nothing to feel, see or hear in the ethereal or -spirit world, these powers would not be possible. And yet the invisible helpers have much to do, even where man is willing to feel, see and hear, to "clear the wires" so that communication can be made possible and practical. The very fact that death draws the bereaved soul into a more active and serious thought of immortality and the spirit world, is an admission that where the treasure is, to quote the saying of Jesus, the heart is also. Immortality deals with life, not death, for life is the greatest contradiction of death. And inasmuch as Spiritualism is a revelation of the life of the spirit, it always seeks to more and more unite spirits in life, and through that union to overcome differences and separations caused first by birth and death, and then by spheres and planes which manifest and express exterior and interior states and conditions of life. This is not impossible, although it is difficult and slow in action and realization.

To commune spiritually as do the saints of the church with the saints on earth, is the blessed and happy privilege of every human being; but this communion, though simple and not always requiring technical knowledge, yet proves in practice that babes in worldly knowledge may yet so venerate and glorify God in a pure, blameless life, that the inner powers declare themselves without effort and freely. The visible helpers silently, patiently, tirelessly, unceasingly assist their loved ones on earth to feel,' see and hear them when they manifest, that is, draw near and speak. And while the body, mind and heart need to be cleansed and purified, they make the ordeal of initiation and purification a joy and not a burden, and so open the way to a free and happy, daily spiritual intercourse. If true marriages are made in heaven, souls are attuned to harmony by celestial messengers. The purer, finer the life, the finer and purer the spirit attractions and spiritual influences. And as clairaudience is an inner, psychic and spiritual power, there is need of a harmonious and peaceful life, before audience can be had with those who dwell in "the heart of the white rose"—the eternal silence.

EXPERIMENT 11

Sit still and listen. Learn to think less and less of material and trivial things and more and more of the spiritual. Listen deeply, divinely, not for sounds or voices, but gentle whispering of the spirit loved ones. Value and learn to value spiritual blessedness above material pleasures.

Go often into the still woods, or the hills and mountains where crowds and vulgar sights never obtrude. Extract the spirit from too close association with the physical senses. Love purity and truth above money. Avoid arguments and so never dispute. Avoid music which, in a subtle way lures the spirit from the silence. Joy in loneliness, if in it saints visit you and minister unto you. Then your loneliness will be ensphered by heavenly and rapturous voices of dear ones gone before. Never doubt but that you will hear. Be of good faith. The deaf shall hear, for spirit can and will commune with spirit.

• • •

12

The Voices And The Voice. Thus Saith The Lord

The Bible as a book of revelation receives its authority from the "thus saith the Lord." Who or what is involved in the sentence is not always made clear. Most students of the Bible are agreed that it was more that the personification of what the Jews held to be ethical or what they accepted as truth. Allegory, metaphor and symbol as well as astrological, occult forms and mystic meanings so abound in all oriental, sacred writings, that what may fittingly describe one situation, episode or section of scripture may be meaningless when applied to other portions of the text. God, Jehovah, Elohim, the Lord, are so common in the Hebrew books, that efforts have been made to identify them as referring to the one Almighty and Eternal God. And yet the plural "gods? surely cannot be made to stand for other words which are singularly or derivatively unique. There is no question but that the unitary conception of deity, the basis of a monotheistic religion, impressed the Egyptian and Assyrian people, from whom the Jews plagarized and idealized many conceptions of their religious and ceremonial, and even ethical beliefs. And yet, Gerald Massey, Herbert Spencer, and noted antiquarians agree that Spiritualism abounds in the Books of the Dead (Egyptian), the Zend Avesta (Persian) and the Hebrew Scriptures. However, mystical references to a plural God may be, these collective words undoubtedly refer to certain rulers of the spiritual world, who at that time appeared and manifested in the human consciousness as lords or masters, and who bore the name of sun gods, because of their association with the puissant, aural light of the ruling spirit of our planetary system. These exalted spirits always appeared to their seers or instruments in a glorious and heavenly light, as is so vividly illustrated in Christ's visitation to Paul.

The Jewish people never denied that their prophets were in communication with the angels and lords of the heavens, called by Paul, the third heaven, the abode of the all glorious, the all pervasive aureola of the Father-Spirit. Still they are now very silent about it, and in their national scriptures very little, except in an extraneous way, is hinted of a once very common practice. The wide spread prevalence and irradicable spiritism of China and Japan, which is practically their national and most ancient religion, despite the fact that Buddhism far outnumbers any other indigenous religion, proves that Spiritualism in a minor or major form platformed all later, concrete developments of ethnic religions. Still this historical fact cannot be made an objection to inner spiritual guidance, or to a metaphysical and moral development of man's nature. Whatever unfoldments of humanity occur, they follow rather than precede revelation. And so divine guidance, in voice or voices through Jehovah or gods is prophetic.

Broadly speaking, the consciousness is the sphere where God speaks. The spirit addresses no physical organ as the ear. The still, small voice, small only because the soul could not live, if the vox dei were expressed in sound waves, is heard in the consciousness, where sound waves do not reach or obtain. And this voice can only be heard, as all spirit voices are heard, clairaudiently.

There is no reason for believing that the story of the reception of the Sinaitic Revelation by Moses was a literally historical fact. Indeed, it detracts in no sense from the value or authority of the Ten Commandments to strip them of allegory and symbolical setting, and transcribe the narrative as an inner rather than an outer revelation of the spirit, who declared himself, in terms of fire and thunder, as "The I AM that I AM." In the material world the soul incarnate lives in the outer world and reaches it through the outer senses. In the spiritual world the soul excarnate lives in the inner world and reaches it through the inner senses. And the whole teaching of religion is that the soul, whether excarnate or incarnate, should obey the voice, rather than the voices, because the vox dei (voice of God) directs the vox populi, (voice of the people). As truth is from within the soul, and not a matter of experience, all spirits should be guided by the one spirit of God, whose word is truth. And we cannot know the truth unless we love it and learn to listen for its revelations, in the consciousness.

EXPERIMENT 12.

Remember that truth is God's omnipresent word, composed of five letters which symbolize the five pointed star, and represents white magic, because the apex is singular and points upward. Seek within for its revealments. It is the key to all mysteries. In every human voice the Divine voice is present. Clairaudiently God speaks through us . "Let the words of my mouth and the meditations of my heart be acceptable." Spirits can use your words, voice and vocal organs, to address you. It is their spirits in breathing upon yours. Watch and wait. Listen and hear.

THE END